NATURE IN THE NEWS

HURRICANE KATRINA

Mary Ann Hoffman

PowerKiDS press.

New York

Published in 2007 by The Rosen Publishing Group, Inc.
29 East 21st Street, New York, NY 10010

Book Design: Daniel Hosek

Photo Credits: Cover, pp. 5, 9 © NOAA/Getty Images, cover (light effect) © Taewoon Lee/Shutterstock; interior texure background © Maja Schon/Shutterstock; pp. 7, 23 © David J. Phillip/AFP/Getty Images; p. 11 © Peter Blottman/Shutterstock; p. 13 © Mark Wilson/Getty Images; p. 15 © Win McNamee/Getty Images; p. 17 © Nathan Holland/Shutterstock; p. 19 © Jim Watson/ AFP/Getty Images; pp. 21, 25, 27 © Mario Tama/Getty Images; p. 29 © Brien Aho/U.S. Navy/ Getty Images.

Library of Congress Cataloging-in-Publication Data

Hoffman, Mary Ann, 1947-
  Hurricane Katrina / Mary Ann Hoffman.
      p. cm. -- (Nature in the news)
  Includes index.
  ISBN-13: 978-1-4042-3537-X
  ISBN-10: 1-4042-3537-X (library binding)
 1. Hurricane Katrina, 2005--Juvenile literature. 2. Disaster victims--Louisiana--New Orleans--Juvenile literature. 3. Disaster relief--Louisiana--New Orleans--Juvenile literature. 4. Rescue work--Louisiana--New Orleans--Juvenile literature. I. Title. II. Series.
  HV636 2005 .U6 H64 2007
  976.3'35064--dc22
                           2006016180

Manufactured in the United States of America

CONTENTS

HURRICANE KATRINA

Hurricane Katrina was one of the worst hurricanes in United States history. It began as a **tropical depression** over the Bahamas in the North Atlantic Ocean on August 23, 2005. The next day it gained strength and became a **tropical storm**. It crossed southern Florida on August 25. It had become even stronger and was now a hurricane.

Katrina's winds had slowed to about 125 miles (201 km) per hour when it made landfall in Louisiana, Mississippi, and Alabama on August 29. However, it was still a powerful storm and caused much **damage**.

This picture from space was taken on August 29, 2005, just as Hurricane Katrina reached Louisiana, Mississippi, and Alabama.

This map shows Katrina's path.

MISSISSIPPI
ALABAMA
LOUISIANA
FLORIDA
ATLANTIC OCEAN
GULF OF MEXICO
BAHAMAS
CARIBBEAN SEA

More than 1 million people left the states along the Gulf of Mexico before Hurricane Katrina hit. They took only the things they could easily move. They left their homes and most of their belongings behind. However, thousands of people did not leave. Many did not have a way to travel. Many were old or sick. Many would not leave their pets behind. Many just did not want to go. Some people went to **official shelters**. Others stayed in their homes. Once Katrina's winds and heavy rainfall began, it was too late to leave. Cities flooded. Power was lost. Water lines broke. Fires started when gas lines broke open. People were trapped.

People climbed onto rooftops as floodwaters caused by Hurricane Katrina got higher.

What Is a Hurricane?

A hurricane is a large tropical storm with spinning winds. Hurricanes begin as thunderstorms over the warm waters of the North Atlantic Ocean in summer and early fall. The temperature of the ocean water usually has to be above 80°F (27°C) for a hurricane to form. The tropical storm picks up warm, moisture-filled air as it moves west. The warm, moist ocean air rises and forms thunderstorms. Groups of thunderstorms move and turn with increasing speed as Earth spins, creating a hurricane. The rotation of Earth causes the winds over the North Atlantic to spin in a **counterclockwise** direction.

This picture of Hurricane Katrina over the Gulf of Mexico was taken from space. ▶

The tropical storm becomes a hurricane when its swirling winds are over 74 miles (119 km) per hour. By this time, the storm has usually formed an "eye" and an "eyewall." The "eye" of the hurricane is at the center of the storm. Around the "eye" is the "eyewall", a band of thick clouds, heavy rains, and strong winds. This is where the hurricane has the most force and power. The winds of the "eyewall" can be more than 200 miles (322 km) per hour!

Around the "eye" are the bands of clouds and powerful winds of the "eyewall".

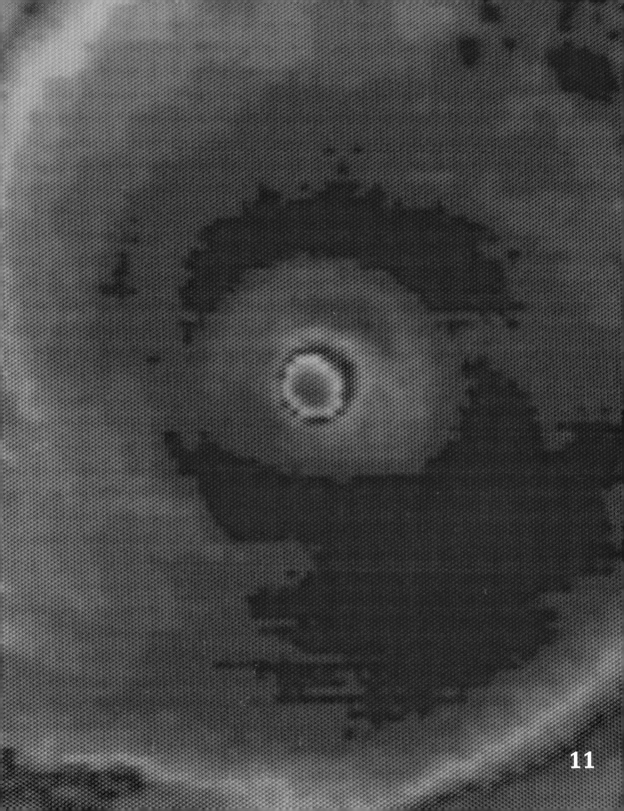

11

WHAT CAN A HURRICANE DO?

Hurricanes can cause great damage when they hit land. Their strong winds can break off tree branches and even uproot trees. They tear the roofs off buildings. They lift cars off the ground. They pull down power lines. The winds send objects flying through the air.

The heavy rain can cause flooding. The ground cannot hold all the water. Rivers quickly rise and flow over their banks, adding to the water already on the ground. Mudslides may occur as wet ground slips away. Communities along the coastlines are also in danger from storm surges. Storm surges occur when strong winds push ocean or lake waters onto the land. A storm surge can be over 30 feet (9 m) high!

A palm tree on Canal Street in New Orleans, Louisiana, was blown over by the strong winds of Hurricane Katrina.

CATEGORIES OF HURRICANES

Hurricane Katrina was a **Category** 3 hurricane when it hit land. Hurricanes are rated on their strength and the damage they may cause. A scale from 1 to 5 is used to help people prepare for hurricanes.

- **Category 1**: Wind speeds of 74 to 95 miles (119 to 153 km) per hour. Some flooding and some damage to trees and buildings.
- **Category 2**: Wind speeds of 96 to 110 miles (154 to 177 km) per hour. Some flooding and tree, roof, window, and power line damage. Mobile homes may suffer a lot of damage.
- **Category 3**: Wind speeds of 111 to 130 miles (178 to 209 km) per hour. Flooding and serious damage to trees and buildings. Mobile homes may be destroyed.
- **Category 4**: Wind speeds of 131 to 155 miles (210 to 249 km) per hour. Severe flooding and serious damage to all types of buildings. Trees blown down. Mobile homes easily destroyed.
- **Category 5**: Wind speeds over 155 miles (249 km) per hour. Severe flooding and loss of buildings. Trees blown down.

This sign was one of the only things left standing in Long Beach, Mississippi, after Hurricane Katrina hit. ▶

15

KATRINA'S POWER

Hurricane Katrina made landfall in Louisiana, Mississippi, and Alabama on August 29, 2005. These Gulf states were not prepared for such a large and powerful hurricane. The high winds, heavy rain, and sheer size of the hurricane caused major loss of life and property. Over 1,600 people died. Property damage costs have been **estimated** to be over $75 billion.

In Mississippi, Gulfport and Biloxi had serious wind and water damage from the 30-foot (9-m) storm surge that destroyed about 90 percent of the buildings along the coast. Mobile, Alabama, was under 2 to 3 feet (.6 to .9 m) of water when the storm surge pushed the water from Mobile Bay onto the land. New Orleans, Louisiana, was flooded when the city's **levee** system broke down.

Cars and homes in Gulfport, Mississippi, were badly damaged by Hurricane Katrina.

This map shows where Gulfport, Biloxi, Mobile, and New Orleans are located.

ALABAMA

MISSISSIPPI

MOBILE

BILOXI

GULFPORT

LOUISIANA

GULF OF MEXICO

NEW ORLEANS

NEW ORLEANS

New Orleans, Louisiana, had many problems during and after Katrina. New Orleans is Louisiana's largest city. It is located on the banks of the Mississippi River, near the Gulf of Mexico. Lake Pontchartrain (PAHN-chur-trayn) is its northern border. The river, the Gulf, and the lake are connected by waterways.

About 80 percent of New Orleans is below **sea level**. It is like a bowl with water surrounding it. The river is about 11 feet (3.4 m) above sea level. The lake is about 2 feet (.6 m) above sea level. There are natural levees or banks of earth along the river and lake. Levees made of sandbags, soil, steel, and **concrete** were built along the river and lake to add to the natural levees. Usually, the levees keep the waters from flooding the land.

This picture shows a flooded New Orleans after the levees broke during Hurricane Katrina.

This map shows the many bodies of water surrounding New Orleans.

LAKE
PONTCHARTRAIN

NEW ORLEANS

MISSISSIPPI RIVER

GULF OF MEXICO

There are **wetlands** along the Mississippi River and Lake Pontchartrain. The wetlands are between the bodies of water and the land. Wetlands lessen the effects of storm surge. Hurricane winds may be reduced as they blow across wetlands. Wetlands soak up floodwaters from the rivers and the lakes. However, the wetlands along the Mississippi River and Lake Pontchartrain have been disappearing.

Building higher levees has stopped the flooding of the muddy river. This flooding added rich soil and had helped maintain the wetlands. Waterways that were cut through the wetlands changed the flow of the river, hurting the wetlands. The wetlands have also been **drained** to make room for the growing population.

Workers built a levee of concrete and steel along a waterway in New Orleans. The levees were built about 14 to 23 feet (4.3 to 7 m) high. ▶

BIG PROBLEMS

A large part of New Orleans was soon underwater from Hurricane Katrina. The hurricane was a Category 3 when it hit New Orleans. The wind and rain made the lake and river waters rise and flow over their banks. The power of the storm broke through levees that were not strong enough or tall enough to hold the water back. Water poured down into the city below. There was nothing to stop it. The streets were soon filled with floodwaters. There was no way for cars or trucks to move. The people who were still in the city had to stay where they were.

The floodwaters from Hurricane Katrina filled the streets of New Orleans. Some parts of the city were under 20 feet (6.2 m) of water.

23

Just before Katrina hit, the people who were still in the city were asked to go to official shelters such as the Superdome or the **convention center**. It was thought that because of the size of these two buildings, people could be cared for and they would be safe. However, between 50,000 and 100,000 people needed a place to go. The leaders and the people who were in charge of the shelters did not expect that many. There was not enough food and water. There were not enough bathrooms. There was not enough room for all the people who came.

Thousands of people waited in line to enter the Superdome before Hurricane Katrina hit. ▶

New Orleans is below sea level, so the floodwaters did not drain away. Eighty percent of the city was underwater. The city was without power. The pumps needed to pump out the floodwaters were damaged in the hurricane. People were forced to stay in the official shelters for several days. It was almost impossible to get more supplies to the shelters because of the damage and flooding.

Since the city was not safe, the people who were in the Superdome, the convention center, and homes needed to be taken out of the city.

People at the Superdome were still waiting to be taken out of the city 4 days after Katrina hit. ▶

27

The city, state, and federal governments did not work well together before, during, or after Hurricane Katrina. The leaders who were in charge did not have a good plan for what needed to happen if a very strong hurricane hit. The city of New Orleans may have been the least prepared. The levee system was not strong enough to hold back the floodwaters. The floodwaters broke through and over the levees. The city was flooded.

Slowly, food, water, and supplies were brought in and given to people. The people who were trapped in New Orleans were finally taken to safer places.

U.S. Navy helicopters, like the one shown, brought water and food to some people waiting to be taken out of New Orleans.

REBUILDING

Some people from Louisiana, Mississippi, and Alabama are still living in other parts of the country, waiting to come back to their cities. Many have returned and are working hard to **rebuild** their cities and their lives.

Billions of dollars in government aid have been given to Louisiana, Mississippi, and Alabama. **Relief agencies** such as the American Red Cross and the Salvation Army as well as **volunteer** groups and individuals have given money, supplies, and time to help with the cleanup and rebuilding. People from around the world have offered aid.

Hurricane Katrina was one of the worst natural disasters in the history of the United States. By looking at what happened before, during, and after Katrina, we can learn the importance of planning and working together.

GLOSSARY

category (KAA-tuh-gohr-ee) A group within a system.

concrete (KAHN-kreet) Hard, strong building matter made from sand, small stones, and other things.

convention center (kuhn-VEHN-shun SEHN-tuhr) A very large building used for large meetings and special events.

counterclockwise (kown-tuhr-KLAHK-wyz) Turning in the opposite direction from the direction that the hands of a clock move.

damage (DAA-mihj) Loss or harm.

drain (DRAYN) To let out water.

estimate (EHS-tuh-mayt) To make an educated guess.

levee (LEH-vee) A raised area along a river or lake to hold back water.

official shelter (uh-FIH-shul SHEL-tuhr) A place set up by authorities that provides food and somewhere to stay.

rebuild (REE-bild) To build again or make repairs.

relief agency (RIH-leef AY-juhn-see) A group that helps people in times of trouble.

sea level (SEE LEH-vuhl) The level of the surface of the ocean.

tropical depression (TRAH-pih-kuhl dih-PREH-shun) A group of thunderstorms that have come together and begun spinning. Wind speeds near the center are 23 to 39 miles (37 to 63 km) per hour.

tropical storm (TRAH-pih-kuhl STOHRM) A storm with high winds and rain but less than hurricane force. A tropical storm has winds over 39 miles (63 km) per hour.

volunteer (VAH-luhn-teer) A person who helps without being asked.

wetland (WEHT-land) A soft, wet area with grasses and small plants.

INDEX

WEB SITES

Due to the changing nature of Internet links, PowerKids Press has developed an online list of Web sites related to the subject of this book. This site is updated regularly. Please use this link to access the list:
http://www.powerkidslinks.com/natnews/katrina/